Bubbles the Dragon and the missing ingredients

By: Jessica Adams

Illustrated By: Andrew and Jessica Adams

Bubbles the dragon and Little Rabbit are going to stay at Grandma Dragon's House this weekend.

Bubbles and rabbit are going to go bake goodies and watch movies with Grandma Dragon.

Grandma Dragon said, "She is going to teach Little Rabbit and Bubbles how to make her famous spotted berry pie."

Spotted Berry Pie

Ingredients

- ❏ Crust
- ❏ Berry Jam
- ❏ Spotted Berries (20)

Grandma Dragon said,"we have the crust and the berry jam.

Oh, No! We are out of
spotted berries.

NO!

NO!

NO!

We can't make spotted berry pie without spotted berries."

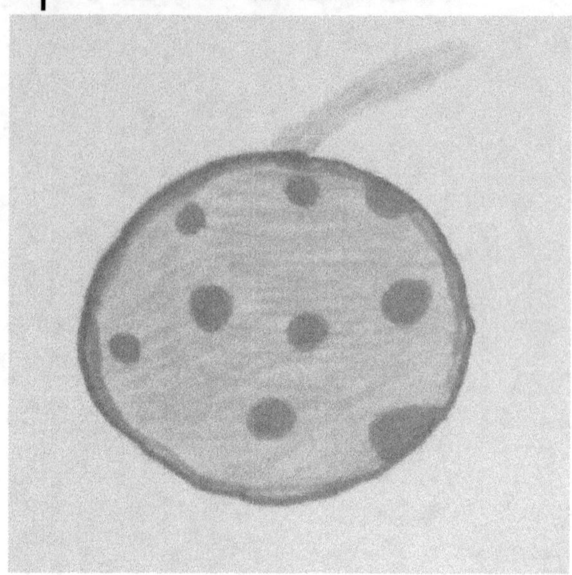

Grandma Dragon sent Little Rabbit and Bubbles the Dragon to berry forest to find the missing spotted berries.

They need twenty spotted berries that match the picture grandma Dragon gave them.

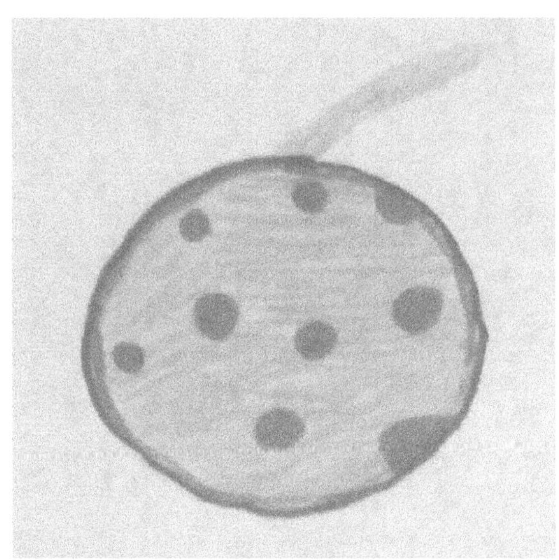

Can you help Bubbles the Dragon and Little Rabbit find and count the spotted berries needed for Grandma Dragon's Recipe?

The spotted berries need to be purple
with red spots and blue stems.

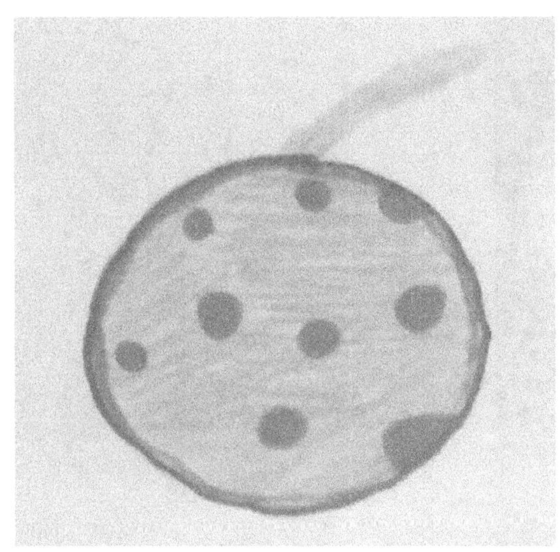

Grandma Dragon gave each one a bucket to carry the spotted berries in.

The spotted berries will be found on the other side of the magical forest in the spotted berry woods.

After walking all through the magical forest, they finally reach spotted berry woods.

Do you see the berries?

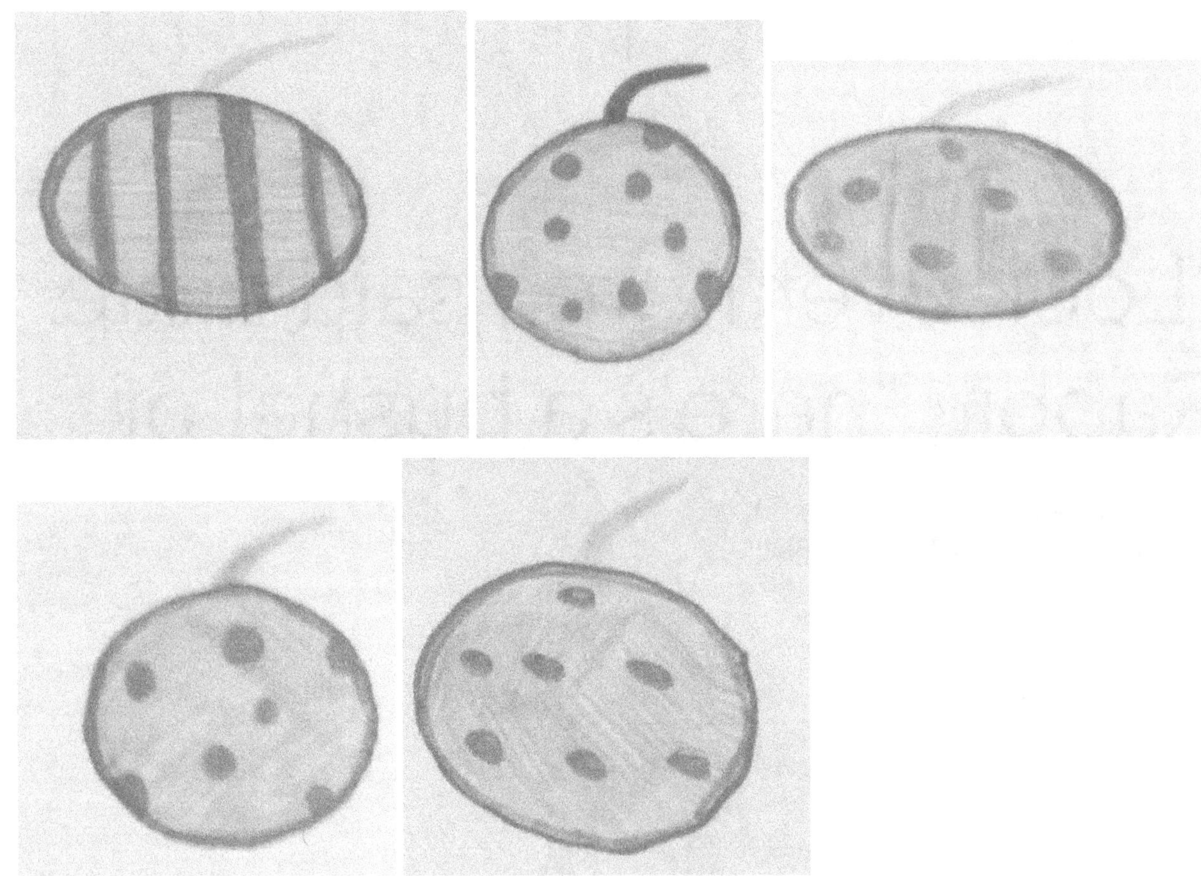

"Look over here", said Little Rabbit, "here's a bushel of berries."

Do these berries match the berry in the picture?

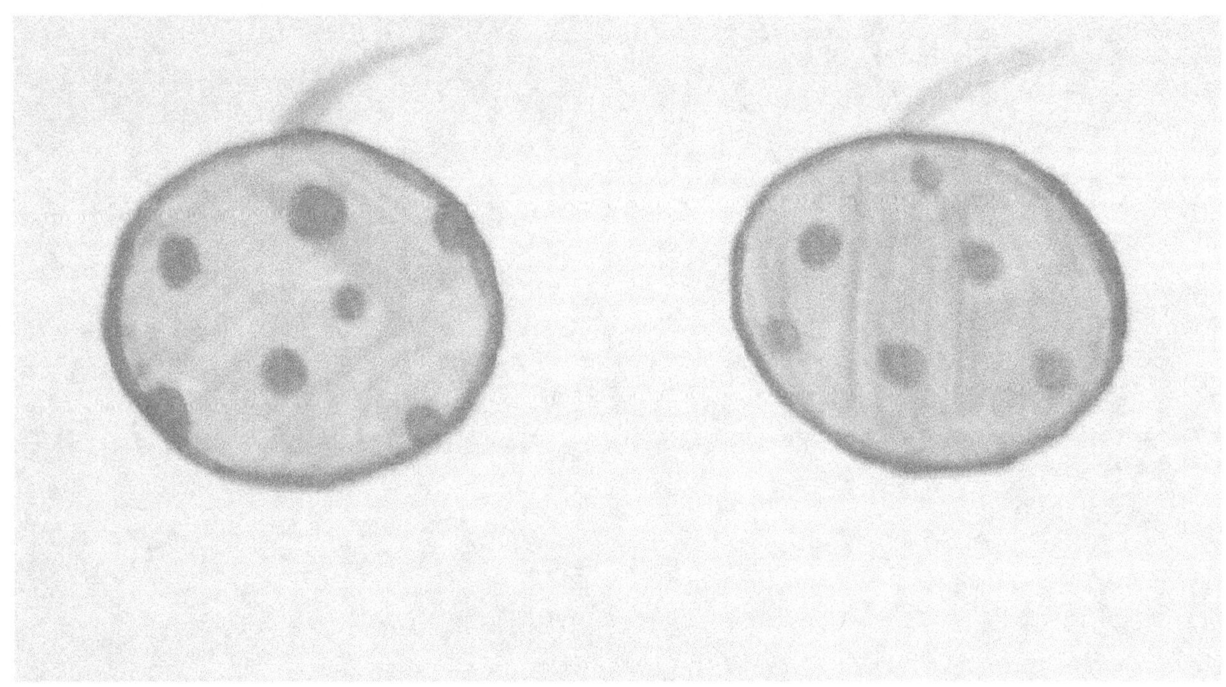

No, these berries are red.

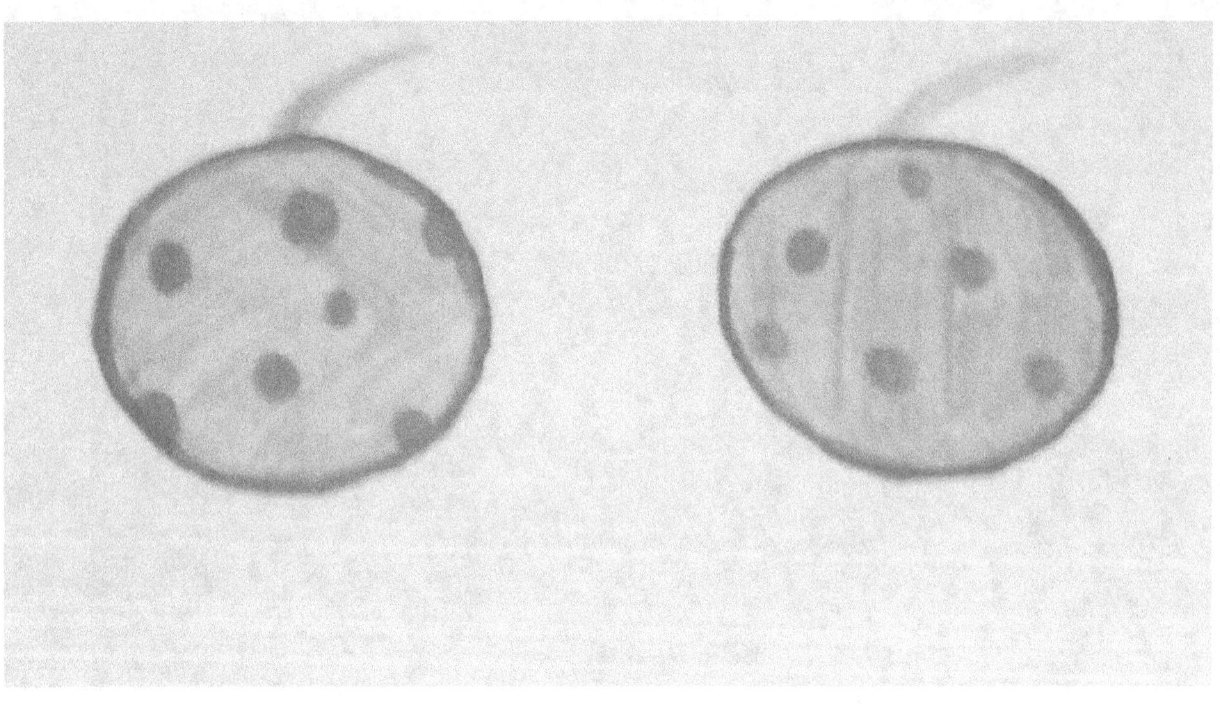

The berry in the picture is purple.

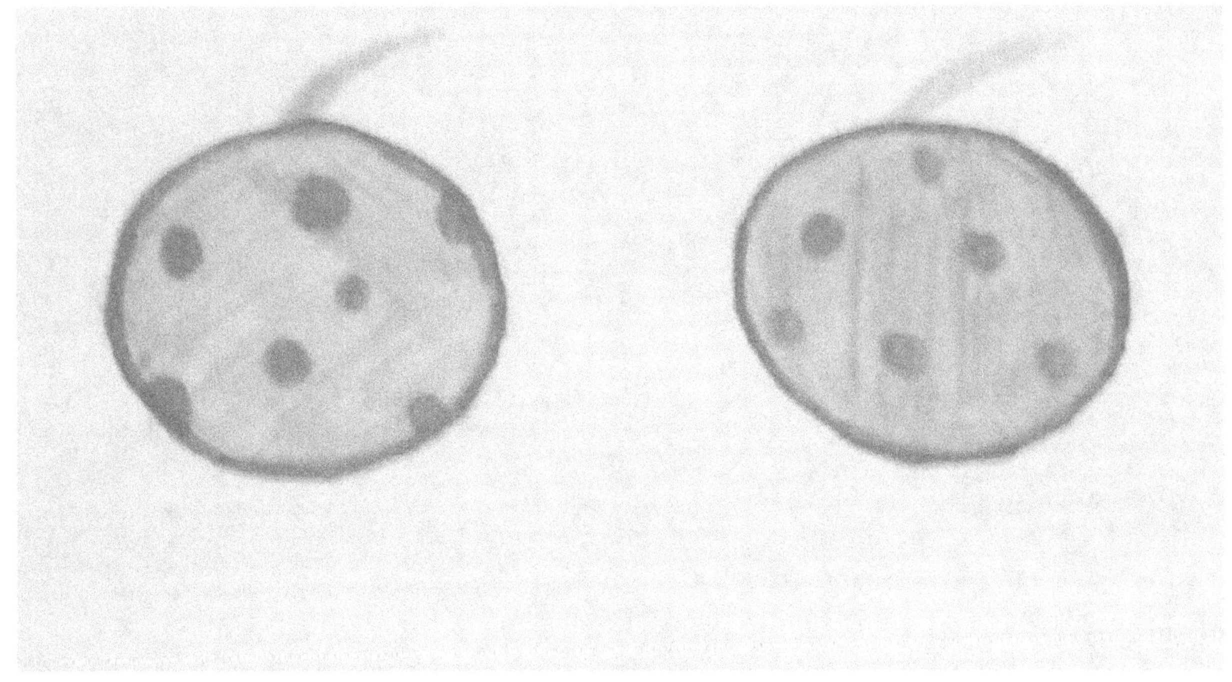

Do you see the spotted berries?

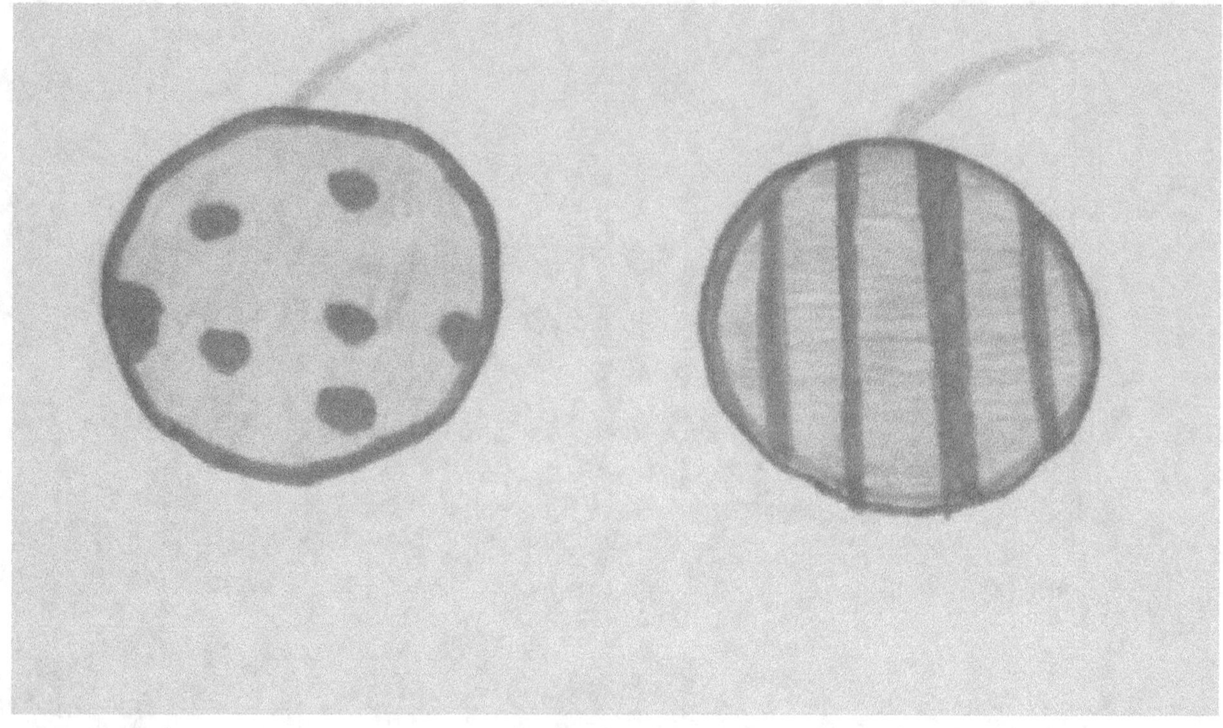

"Look over here",
said Bubbles the
Dragon.
"Here's a bushel of
berries."

Do these berries match the berry in the picture?

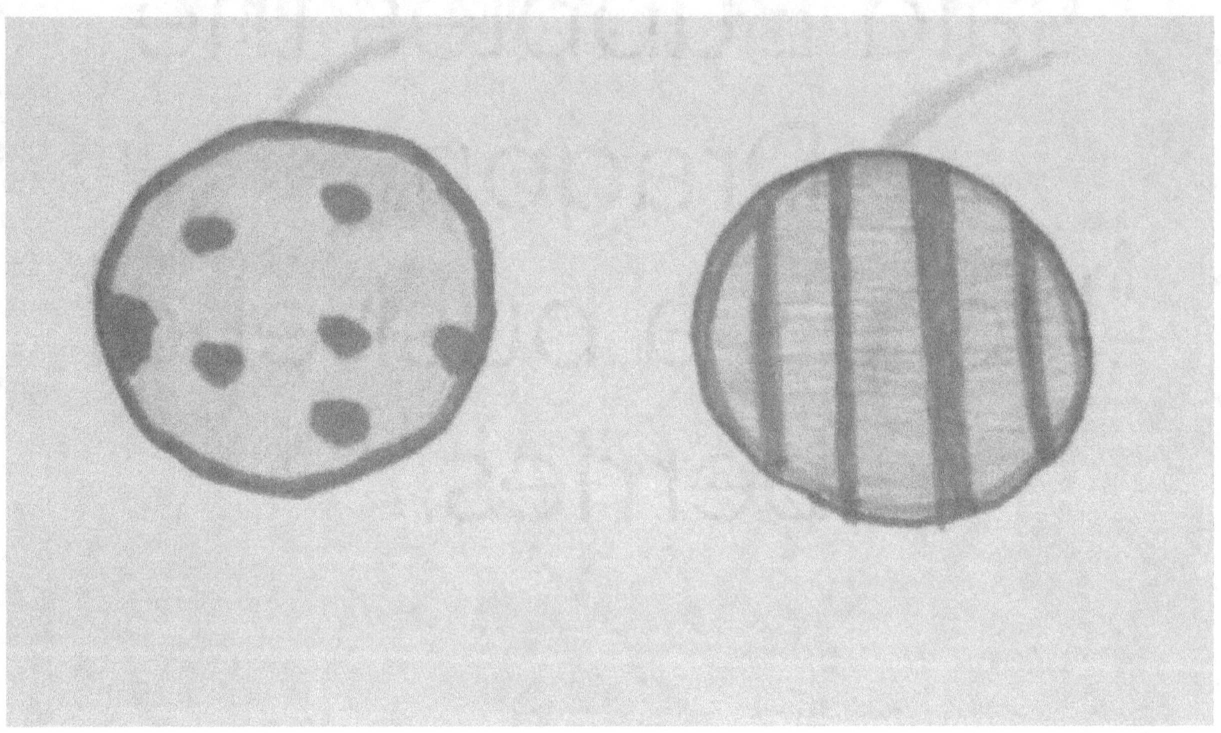

No, these berries have stripes.

This berry in the picture has spots.

Do you see the right spotted berries?

"Look over here", said Little Rabbit.
"Here's a bushel of berries."

Do these berries match the berry in the picture?

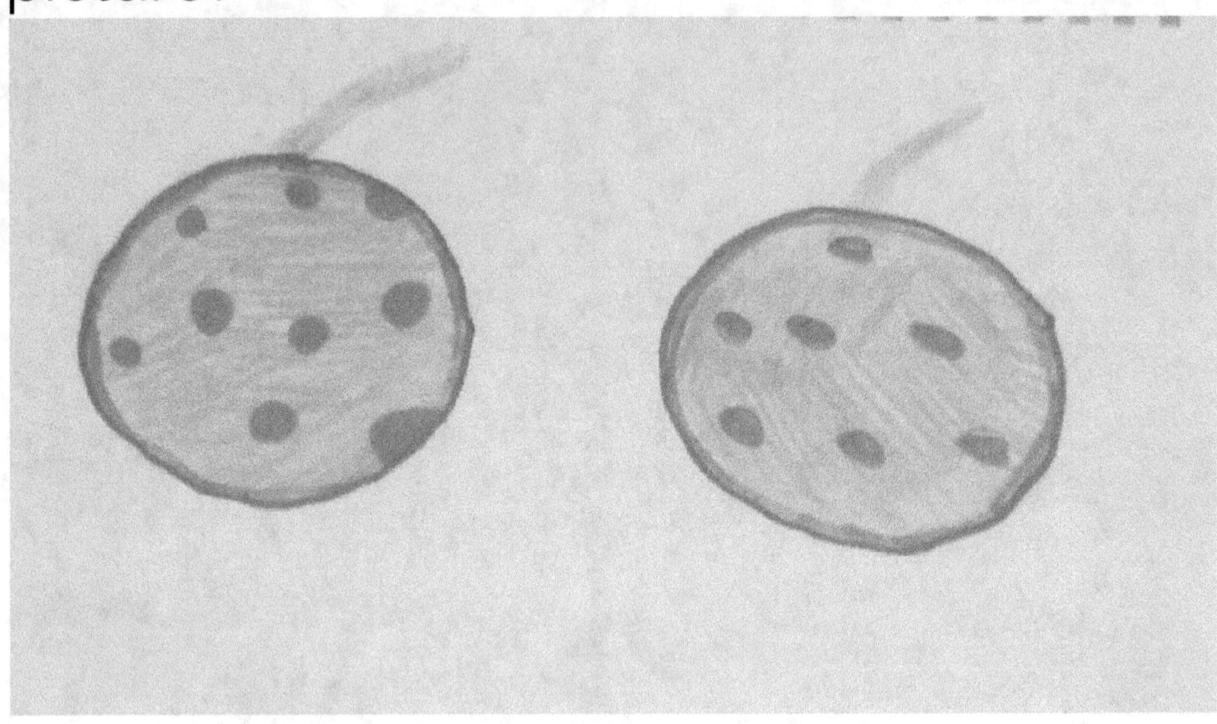

No, these berries have green spots.

The berry in the picture has red spots.

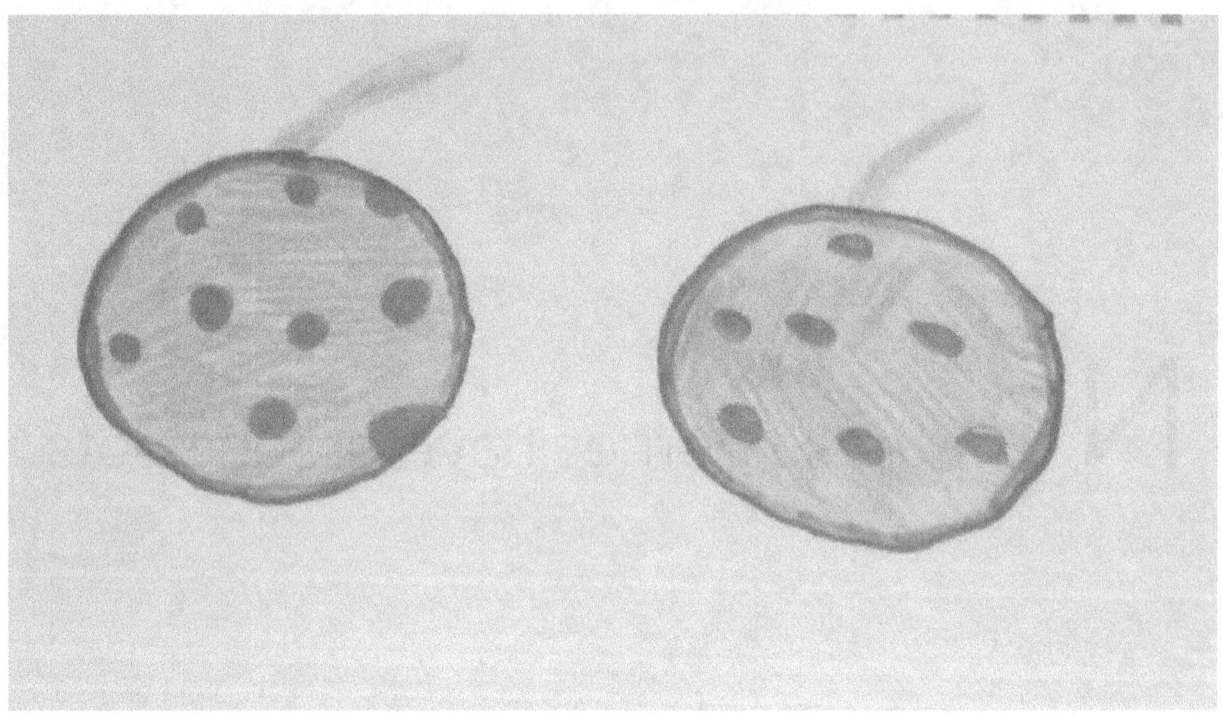

Do you think you see the right berries for Grandma Dragon's Pie?

"Look over here", said Bubbles the Dragon.
"Here's a bushel of berries."

Do these berries match the berry in the picture?

No, these berries have black stems.

The berry in the picture has a blue stem.

Do you see the berries we need?

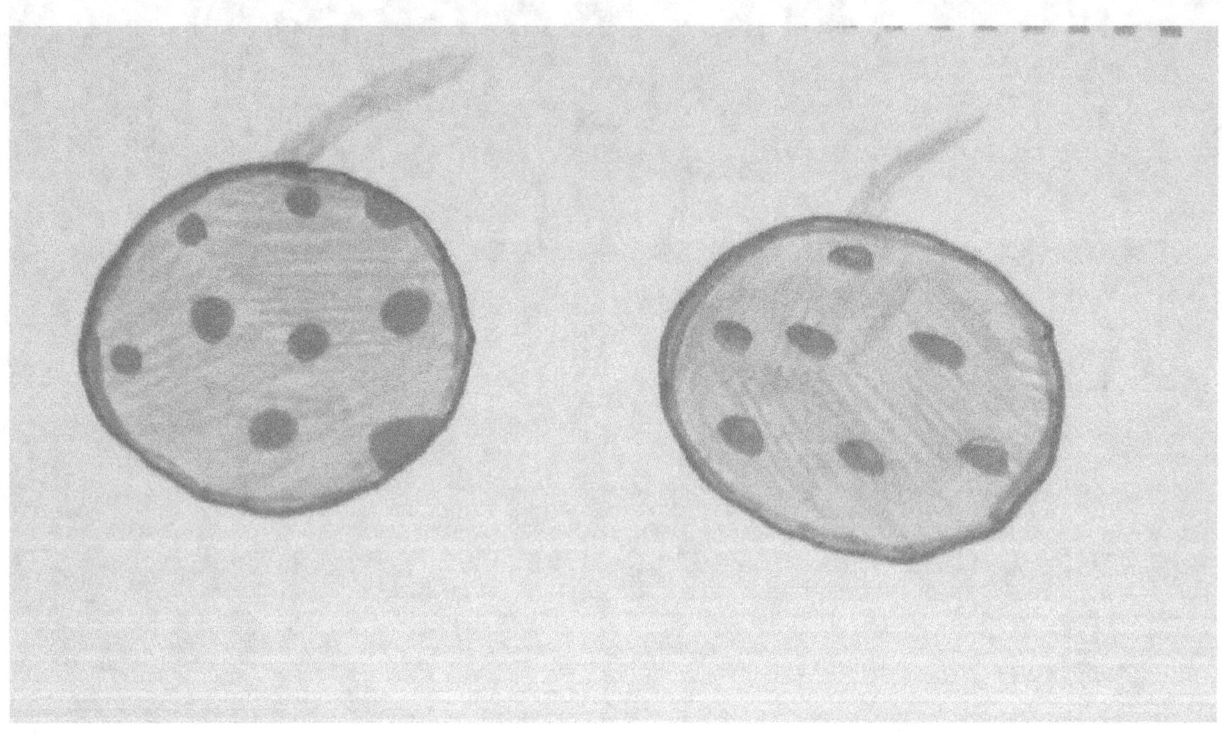

Look over here",said Little Rabbit.
"Here's a bushel of berries."

Do these berries match the berry in the picture?

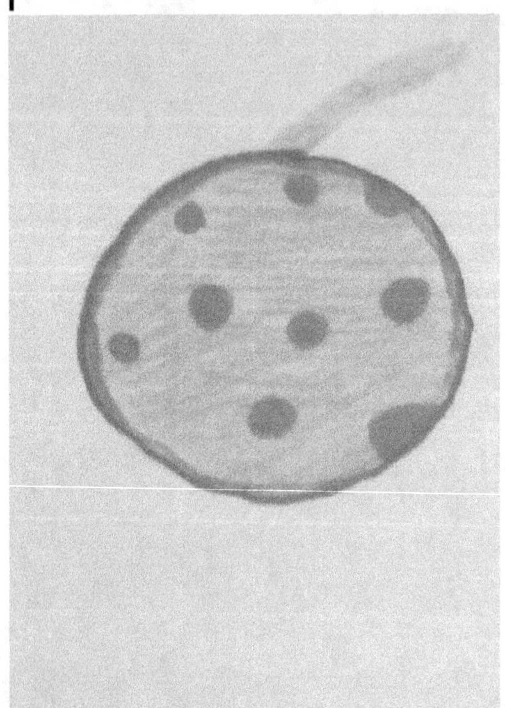

YES THEY DO!!!!!!

These berries are purple with red spots and blue stems.

Bubbles the Dragon and Little Rabbit
have found the missing spotted berries.

How many did Grandma Dragon say
they needed for her spotted berry pie?

Bubbles the Dragon dropped the picture of the spotted berry.

When he picked it up, there was a message on the back from Grandma Dragon.

It said, "we need twenty spotted berries
for my famous spotted berry pie

20

If we have two baskets, how many will go in each basket?

First Let's count to twenty

1,2,3,4,5,6,7,8,9,10

Keep counting.....

11,12,13,14,15

Almost done......

16,17,18,19, and 20

Well lets see what numbers make 20.

What about 5 and 5
5+5=?(20)

NO

5+5=10

10 is close, but it's not 20.

Lets try 10 and 5

10+5=?(20)

NO

10+5=15

15 was closer but still not 20.

Lets try 10 and 10

10+10=?(20)

Yes

10+10=20
And
10 x 2= 20

10 x 2= 20

This is 10 berries each and 2 animals= 20 berries altogether

10 for Little Rabbit +
10 for Bubbles =
20 berries for Grandma Dragon's Pie

Lets count by twos !

2,4,6,8,10

Good let's keep counting to twenty.

12,14,16,18,20

Little rabbit and Bubbles picked 10 spotted berries for their baskets.

20

They collected all twenty berries and went back to Grandma Dragon's house.

Grandma Dragon was so happy that they were able to find the spotted berries for her famous pie.

Grandma Dragon prepared the pie crust.

Can you help Bubble and Little Rabbit count and put the berries in the crust.

Let's count by fives this time.....

5,10, 15, 20, done

Last Grandma Dragon poured the berry jam over the spotted berries and placed it in the oven for heating.

Bubbles the Dragon setup the movie.

Little Rabbit gathered plates,cups, and silverware.

Grandma Dragon pulled out the famous spotted berry pie.

Would you like to join them for a slice of spotted berry pie,a glass of milk and a movie?

Bubbles and Little rabbit had a great time at Grandma Dragons house.

I think Bubbles might have had too much of Grandma's spotted berry pie.

We hope you had fun with us on our search for spotted berries and our movie and snack.

Thank you for all your help searching, counting, and having fun with us.